THE NEW MELUSINA

BY

JOHANN WOLFGANG VON GOETHE

British Library Cataloguing-in-Publication Data
A catalogue record for this book is available from
the British Library

Contents

Johann Wolfgang Von Goethe

Johann Wolfgang Von Goethe was born Frankfurt, Germany in 1749. His early education was inconsistent, ranging from home tutoring to informal lessons with his father, but at a young age he developed an excellent grasp of European languages. Upon turning sixteen, and on his father's wishes, Goethe went to Leipzig University to study law. However, he had already developed a deep passion for writing, and gained some recognition in his teens for his output of lyric poetry.

In 1770, Goethe continued his law studies in Strasbourg, where he also attended lectures on a range of topics. During this period, he met daily with the philosopher and theologian Johann Gottfried Herder, who had a great effect on his work. Goethe published his first anthology of poems, *Neue Lieder in Melodien gesetzt von B.T.Breitkopf,* in 1770, before returning to Frankfurt to practice law. Four years later, he published *Die Leiden des jungen Werthers* (*The Sorrows of Young Werther*) (1774). Overnight, the novel became the biggest bestseller of its time, propelling Goethe into international fame. Less than a year later, he was invited to Weimar by Duke Karl August, where he stayed for the majority of the rest of his life, producing melodramas, operettas, and plays to entertain the court.

In 1787, Goethe published his well-known *Ipigenie auf Tauris* (*Ipigenie in Tauris*), and four years later was conferred his title of nobility, 'von Goethe', by Emperor Joseph II. It was also around this time that, as a result of his studies of the human anatomy, Goethe discovered the human intermaxillary bone. He even found time to climb Mount Vesuvius in Naples, Italy, and start work on what would become his masterpiece, *Faust.* In 1795, he published the novel *Wilhelm Meisters Lehrjahre* (*Wilhelm Meister's Apprenticeship*), seen by many modern critics as the first *Bildungsroman.*

The first part of *Faust* was published in 1808, the same year that Goethe met with Napoleon Bonaparte, a great fan of his work. He finished the second part more than twenty years later, in 1831. Now regarded as one of the greatest works of German literature of all time, the tragic play wasn't published in full until after Goethe's somewhat unexpected death in March of 1832. He now rests in the Historic Cemetery in Wiemar.

The New Melusina

Johann Wolfgang von Goethe

(1749-1832)

Honoured Gentlemen: Since I know you care very little for introductory remarks or preambles, I shall at once assure you that this time I hope to conduct myself in a highly proper manner. I admit that in the past I have given out many true stories which have proved highly satisfactory to everyone; but today I boldly assert that I have one to relate which far surpasses all previous tales; one which, although it happened to me several years ago, still makes me uneasy whenever I remember it, awakening the hope for some final resolution. It would be hard for you to match it.

Before all, it must be confessed that I have not always so planned my life as to insure my immediate future, or even my next day. In my youth I was not a good manager, and often found myself in various straits. Once I set out upon a journey which should have been highly profitable; but I cut my cloth too big, and after starting out in a private post-chaise had to continue in the public stagecoach, till at last I was obliged to face the rest of the way on foot.

Being a quick-witted fellow, I had made a custom of seeking out the landlady, or even the cook, as soon as I came to an inn, and by treating them to a little flattery I usually succeeded in reducing my expenses. One evening as I was entering the post-tavern of a small town, intent on pursuing my usual practice, a handsome, two-seated carriage, drawn by four horses, rattled up to the door behind me. I turned and saw a solitary young woman, unattended by a maid or servants. I made haste to open the door for her and to ask if I could be of service. As she stepped out she disclosed a beautiful figure and, on closer inspection, an amiable countenance marked by faint though not unpleasant traces of sadness. Again I inquired if I could in any way serve her. 'Oh, yes,' she said, 'if you will lift out the little casket that lies on the seat and carry it in for me; but, I entreat you, hold it level and do not shift or shake it in the slightest degree.' I took up the casket cautiously, she closed the carriage door, we ascended the steps together and she told the servants that she would remain overnight.

Now we were alone in the room; she directed me to place the casket on the table which stood near the wall, and inferring from certain of her movements that she wished to be alone, I took my leave, kissing her hand respectfully but ardently.

At that she said: 'Order supper for us both,' and I leave you to imagine with what satisfaction I carried out her bidding, so exalted that I scarcely deigned to glance at the landlady or the servants. Impatiently I waited for the moment that would bring me to her once more. Supper was served, we sat facing each other. For the first time in quite a while I regaled myself with a good meal and at the same time with a charming sight: indeed, it seemed to me that she became more beautiful with every minute.

Her conversation was engaging, yet she sought to reject everything pertaining to attraction or love. The table was cleared; I tarried, I tried every dodge to approach her -- but in vain. She held me off with a certain dignity I could not withstand; indeed, against my will I was forced to leave her rather early.

After a night spent mostly in wakefulness, or filled with restless dreams, I arose early and asked whether the horses had been ordered. Upon being told 'No,' I walked into the garden where I saw her standing dressed at her window. I hastened to go up to her. As she came towards me, as beautiful, no, more beautiful than yesterday, I was suddenly overcome by desire, cunning and audacity; I rushed towards her and clasped her in my arms. 'Heavenly, irresistible creature,' I cried, 'forgive me, but it is impossible to withstand you!' With unbelievable agility she released herself before I had the chance even to press a kiss upon her cheek. 'Restrain yourself from such sudden and passionate outbreaks, unless you want to forego a bit of good fortune that lies near you, but which can be obtained only after certain tests.'

'Exact of me what you will, angelic spirit,' I exclaimed, 'but do not drive me to despair.' She smiled as she answered: 'If you wish to devote your services to me, hear the conditions. I came here to visit a woman friend and to spend a few days with her; meanwhile I would like my carriage and this little case to be brought further along the road. Would you care to undertake this? You will have nothing to do but to lift the case in and out of the carriage, to sit beside it and to be responsible for it. When you come to an inn you are to place it in a room by itself, in which you will neither sit nor sleep. You will lock the room each time with this key, which opens and closes every lock, and has the power of making it impossible for the lock to be opened by any-one in the meantime.'

I looked at her, overcome by a feeling of strangeness; I promised her I would do everything if only I might hope to see her soon again, and if she would seal this hope by a kiss. She did so, and from that moment I became wholly her own. She told me that now I should order the horses. We discussed the road I should take as well as the places where I was to stop and await her. Finally she pressed a purse of gold into my hand, and I a kiss upon hers. At parting she seemed to be moved, and I was past knowing what I was doing or was about to do.

After I had given the order, I came back and found the door of the room locked. I tested my master-key and it performed perfectly. The door sprang open, the room was empty save for the casket which stood on the table where I had placed it.

The carriage had drawn to the door; I took down the casket solicitously and placed it beside me. The housekeeper asked, 'But where is the lady?' and a child answered: 'She went into the town.' I took leave of the servants and drove off as it were in triumph, from the place where but last evening I had arrived with dust-covered leggings. You may take it for granted that now, completely at leisure, I reviewed the whole matter, counted the money, made all sorts of plans and occasionally glanced over at the casket, I kept straight on, passing several places, and did not halt until I reached the fair-sized town where she had directed me to meet her. Her commands were scrupulously obeyed; the casket was placed in a room by itself and a couple of wax candles lighted near it, just as she had ordered. I locked the room, got to rights in mine, and made myself fairly comfortable.

For a while I was engrossed in thoughts of her, but very soon time hung heavy on my hands. I was unaccustomed to living without companionship and presently I found some to my taste at the inn tables and in public places. Under these circumstances my money began to melt away, and one evening when I had recklessly yielded to a passionate fit of gambling it vanished completely from my purse. On coming back to my room I was beside myself. Without funds, while to all appearances a rich man, with the prospect of a heavy debt, uncertain as to whether or when my lovely one would show up, I was in the greatest dilemma. Now my longing for her was doubled, and I was convinced I could no longer live without her and her money.

After supper, for which I had little appetite, since now I was forced to eat alone, I paced quickly to and fro in my room, talking aloud to myself, upbraiding myself, throwing myself on the floor, tearing my hair and behaving in a most unruly fashion. Of a sudden I hear a soft movement in the locked room adjoining, and shortly after a knock on the well-guarded door. I pull myself together, reach for the master-key; but the folding-doors spring open of themselves, and in the gleam from the lighted tapers my lovely one approaches. I throw myself at her feet, kissing her dress, her hand; she raises me, but I lack courage to embrace her, almost to look at her; yet frankly though ruefully I confess my fault. 'It is pardonable,' she said, 'only, alas, you delay your own good fortune as well as mine. Now you must again cover some ground in the world before we meet again. Here is more gold, and it will suffice if you are disposed to be the least bit prudent. But if wine and women have proved your undoing this time, protect yourself henceforth from both, and let me hope for a happy reunion.'

She stepped back through the doorway, the folding-doors closed, I knocked, I entreated, but nothing more could be heard. Next morning when I asked for my account, the young waiter smiled and said: 'We know all right why you lock your doors in so artful and baffling a way that no master-key is able to open them. Our guess was that you had a lot of money and valuables; but now your treasure has been seen coming down the stairs, and from all accounts it appeared worth being well-guarded.'

To this I made no answer, but settling my account I entered the carriage with my casket. Once again I drove into the wide world, firmly resolved that in future I would heed the warning of my mysterious friend. Yet, almost as soon as I arrived at a large town I made the acquaintance of some affable young women from whom I was utterly unable to tear myself away. They, it seemed, wished me to pay dearly for their favour, for although they constantly kept me at a distance, they led me from one expense to the other. And as I sought only to advance their pleasure, I never gave a second thought to my purse, but continued to give out and to spend whenever occasion arose. Consequently, I was astonished and overjoyed when, after a few weeks, I noticed that my purse showed no signs of shrinkage but was as bulky and bulging as at first. Since I wanted to make sure of this charming trait, I sat down to count up what I had, made a note of the precise amount, and began to live with my companions as gaily as before.

There were plenty of excursions by land and water, also dancing and other pleasures, but now no great attention was called for to perceive that the purse was indeed dwindling, as if, through my deuced counting, I had filched from it the virtue of being uncountable. Meanwhile, the life of pleasure being in full swing I could not back out, even though I was soon at the end of my cash. I cursed my state, calling out upon my friend for having led me into temptation, taking it ill of her that she failed to put in an appearance; angrily I declared myself free of all duties towards her and considered opening the casket on the chance that some help might be found in it. For, although it was not quite heavy enough to contain gold, yet it might hold jewels, and these too would be welcome. I was about to carry out my intention but decided to postpone it until the night, in order to undertake the operation in utter quiet, and ran off to a banquet which was just beginning. Things there were going full tilt and we were stirred up by the wine and the blaring of the trumpets when a stroke of ill-luck befell me: at dessert, a former friend of my favourite beauty returned unexpectedly from a journey, and sitting down beside her attempted with very little formality to claim his old privileges. This gave rise to ill-humour, disputes and brawling. We drew our swords, and I was carried home half dead from several wounds.

The surgeon had bandaged me and left; it was already late in the night and my attendant asleep, as the door of the next room opened and my mysterious friend entered and seated herself beside my bed. She asked how I was; I did not answer, for I was worn and vexed. She went on speaking with much sympathy, rubbed my temples with a certain balsam, so that soon I felt decidedly stronger – so strong that I was able to arouse my anger and to chide her. Speaking impetuously, I threw all the blame for my misfortune upon her, on the passion she had awakened in me, on her appearance and her disappearance, on the tedium and on the longing that had been my portion. I became more and more violent, as though attacked by fever, and finally I swore to her that if she would not be mine, that if this time she refused to belong to me and be united with me, I had no further desire to live. And what is more, I demanded a decisive answer. As she hesitated, fencing with an explanation, I grew quite beside myself, and tore the double and triple bandages from my wounds with the fixed intention of bleeding to death. But how astonished I was when I found my wounds entirely healed, my body spruce and shining, and her in my arms!

We were now the happiest couple in the world. We asked each other's pardon without rightly knowing why. She promised now to travel with me, and soon we were sitting side by side in the carriage with the casket opposite in the place of a third person. I had never made any allusion to it, and even now it did not occur to me to speak of it to her, although there it stood, right before our eyes, and both of us, as occasion required, took charge of it as by an unspoken agreement, save that it was I who always lifted it in and out of the carriage and, as before, attended to locking the doors.

As long as still something remained in the purse I continued to do the paying; when my cash gave out I let her know it. 'That is easy to provide,' she said, and pointed to a pair of small pockets attached at both sides to the top of the carriage, which I had undoubtedly noticed before, but had never used. She reached into one and drew out a few gold pieces, and from the other several silver coins, thus showing me it was possible for us to continue spending as much as we liked. In this way we journeyed from town to town, from country to country, happy either

11

to be by ourselves or with others, and it never occurred to me that she could leave me again, all the less so since for some time past she had certain hopes which would only add to our happiness and our love. But, alas, there came a morning when I found she was not there, and since a sojourn without her was irksome to me, I took my casket and started to travel, tried out the powers of both pockets and found that they still held good.

The journey prospered, and if until now I had not reflected much on my adventure, since I expected these strange happenings to unravel themselves quite naturally yet now something occurred which cast me into a state of astonishment, yes, even of fear. In order to get far away from a place it was my habit to travel day and night, and so it happened that often I drove in the dark, and if accidentally the lamps gave out, my carriage was in total blackness. Once on such a murky night I fell asleep, and on awakening saw the glimmer of a light on the ceiling of my carriage. I observed it and found that it came out of the casket which, because of the hot, dry weather of advancing summer, seemed to have sprung a rift. Again I started to speculate about the jewels; I fancied a carbuncle lying in the box and wished to make sure of it. Twisting myself around as well as I was able, I brought my eye in direct contact with the opening. But how great was my astonishment when I looked into a room brightly lit with candles and furnished with much taste, even magnificence, exactly as if I were looking down from an aperture in the ceiling into a drawing-room of royalty. It is true that I could see only a part of the room, but from that I could surmise the rest. An open fire seemed to be burning on the hearth and near it stood an arm-chair. I held my breath and continued looking. Meanwhile a young woman with a book in her hand approached from the other side of the room, and immediately I recognized her as my wife, although her figure had shrunk to the smallest proportions. The beautiful creature seated herself in the chair near the fireplace to read, and as she arranged the logs with the neatest pair of tongs I could plainly see that this most adorable of little beings was about to become a mother. Now, however, I found it necessary to move slightly from my uncomfortable position, and immediately after, just as I was on the point of looking in again to convince myself that it had not been a dream, the light went out and I peered into blank darkness.

My amazement and terror can easily be imagined. I formed a thousand theories about this discovery, and yet I could think out nothing. In this turmoil I fell asleep and when I awoke I believed I had only dreamed it all. Yet I felt somewhat estranged from my lovely one, and although I carried the casket with ever greater care, I knew not whether her reappearance in full human dimensions was more to be dreaded than desired.

After a while, towards evening, my lovely one actually came to me, dressed in white, and as the room was just getting dark she seemed taller to me than she usually appeared, and I remembered having heard that all from the race of pixies and gnomes noticeably increase in stature with the coming of night. She rushed into my arms as she always did, but I was unable to clasp her to my uneasy breast with complete joy.

'My dearest,' she said, 'the way you receive me confirms me in feeling what I, alas, already know. You have seen me in the interval; you have learned of the state in which at certain times I find myself. This causes a break in your happiness and also in mine, which indeed is on the point of being utterly destroyed. I must leave you, and I do not know if I shall ever see you again.' Her presence, the charm with which she spoke, at once removed nearly all recollection of that sight which even before had appeared in my mind's eye like a dream. Impulsively I embraced her, convinced her of my passion, assured her of my innocence and told her the accidental nature of my discovery; in short, I did everything that seemed to quiet her and she in turn tried to bring me calm.

'Test yourself thoroughly,' she said, 'to see whether this discovery has not marred your love, whether you can forget that I live with you in two forms, and whether the diminution in my person will not diminish your affection as well.'

I looked at her; she was more beautiful than ever, and I thought to myself: 'Is it then such a great misfortune to possess a wife who from time to time becomes a pygmy, so that one can carry her around in a box? Would it not be far worse were she to become a giantess and clap her husband into the box?' My serenity returned. Not for anything in the world would I have let her go. 'Dear heart,' I answered, 'let us remain and continue to be as we have been. Could we find anything more delightful? Consult your own comfort, and I promise to carry the casket all the more carefully. How could I retain a bad impression from the prettiest spectacle I have ever seen in my whole life? How happy all lovers, could they possess such miniature pictures! And after all it was merely such a picture, a little conjuring trick. You are just sounding me, teasing me; however you shall see how I shall acquit myself.'

'The matter is graver than you think,' said the lovely creature; 'meanwhile I am quite content that you take it so lightly; for it may still turn out quite happily for us both. I shall trust to you, and for my part I shall do whatever is possible; only promise me never to think back on this discovery with reproach. In addition, I earnestly beg you to beware more than ever of anger and of wine.'

I promised what she desired; I would have gone on promising anything and everything; but she herself changed the subject and everything ran smoothly as before. There was no reason for us to move from the place where we were staying; the town was large, the society varied, the season favourable for country jaunts and garden parties.

At all such festivities my wife was greatly in demand, much sought after by both men and women. A kind and ingratiating manner together with a certain nobility made her loved and respected by everyone. Moreover, she played brilliantly on the lute, accompanying her own singing, and there was never a social evening but must be graced with her talent.

I may as well admit I have never derived a great deal from music; on the contrary, its effect upon me was often unpleasant. Therefore my lovely one, who had observed my reactions in this respect, never tried so to entertain me when we were alone; however, she seemed to find compensation for this when in company where she usually found a host of adorers.

And now – why should I deny it? – our last conversation had not sufficed entirely to dispel the matter, notwithstanding my best intentions; rather had it induced in me an unwonted sensitivity of feeling of which I was not wholly aware. So one evening at a large gathering my restrained ill-humour burst forth, which redounded to my great disadvantage.

Looking back upon the matter dispassionately, I acknowledge that I loved my charmer far less after that unhappy discovery, and now I was becoming jealous of her, a feeling which was new to me. This particular evening as we sat at table, diagonally across though fairly far from one another, I found myself quite content with both my supper-partners, a couple of young women whom for some time past I had found most attractive. What with jesting and sentimental sallies, we were not sparing of the wine; meanwhile at the other side of the table, a pair of music lovers had managed to persuade my wife, and to encourage and lead on the guests to participate in singing, both solo and in Chorus. The two amateurs seemed importunate; the singing made me irritable, and when they demanded that even I should sing a solo stanza, I became really enraged, drained my glass and banged it on the table.

Although the charms of my neighbours soon calmed me again, still it is a bad thing for anger to get out of control. I boiled inwardly, although everything was conducive to pleasure and relaxation. On the contrary, I grew still more petulant when, a lute having been brought, my lovely one accompanied her song to every one else's admiration. Unfortunately, a general silence was requested. This put an end to my chatter, while the sounds set my teeth on edge. Was it any wonder then that the smallest spark set off the mine?

The singers had barely finished a song amid the greatest applause when she looked over to me most lovingly. Unhappily, her glance did not reach my heart. She observed that I gulped down my glass of wine and filled it up again. She warned me affectionately by wagging the forefinger of her right hand. 'Remember it is wine!' she said, just loud enough for me to hear. 'Water is for nixies!' I exclaimed. 'Ladies,' she called to my supper partners, 'Encircle the goblet with every enchantment, so that it is not emptied so often.' 'Surely you will not let yourself be dictated to!' whispered one of them in my ear. 'What's the imp after?' I called out, with an impetuous movement that overturned my glass. 'A great deal is being wasted here!' cried the exquisite creature, plucking the strings of her lute as if to distract the attention of the company from this disturbance and draw it once more to herself. She actually succeeded in doing so, all the more as she stood up, but only as if to play with more comfort, and continued her prelude.

When I saw the red wine flowing over the table-cloth I came to my senses. I realized the great mistake I had made, and was inwardly repentant. For the first time music spoke to me. Her opening stanza was a friendly leave-taking from the company while they could still feel themselves together; with the one following the gathering seemed on the point of flowing apart; everyone felt himself alone, cut off; no one believed himself to be any longer present. But then, what should I say of the last stanza? It was addressed to me alone: the voice of offended love, bidding good-bye to ill-humour and presumption.

I led her home without a word, expecting nothing pleasant for myself. Yet, scarcely were we in our room when she proved herself most kind and charming, yes, even arch, making me the happiest of men.

The following morning, wholly solaced and full of love, I said: 'Many a time you have sung, challenged to do so by good company, as for instance last night when you sang that touching song of farewell; now once, for my sake, sing a pretty and joyful song of welcome in this morning hour, so that it may seem as if we were learning to know each other for the first time.'

'That, my friend, I may not do,' she answered gravely. 'Last night's song made allusion to our parting which must take place at once; for I can only tell you that the way you have violated your promise and your oath will result in calamity for us both: you lightly spurn a great gift of fortune, and even I must renounce my dearest wishes.'

When, at this, I pressed her and pleaded with her to explain herself more clearly, she replied: 'Unhappily, that is easy for me to do, since in any case the possibility of my remaining with you is over. Hear, then, what I would have preferred to conceal from you until our last moments together. The form in which you espied me in the little casket is really congenital and natural to me; for I am a lineal descendant of King Eckwald, the mighty prince of elves, of whom authentic history has so much to tell. As of old, our people are still active and industrious, and there-fore easy to govern as well. But do not assume that the elves have remained backward in respect to their labours. Were this so their most famous products would still be swords which are able to pursue the enemy after whom they are thrown, chains which bind invisibly, mysteriously impenetrable shields, and things of this sort. Instead their principal occupation now is making articles of convenience and adornment, in which they excel all other people on the earth. You would be amazed were you to pass through our workshops and warehouses. All of this would be highly satisfactory, had not a strange circumstance arisen which affected the whole nation, but before all the royal family.'

As she held back momentarily, I requested her to tell me more of these prodigious secrets, to which she complied.

'It is well known,' she said, 'that directly after God had created the world, when the soil was still dry and the mountains stood there mighty and majestic, that God, I say, pro-ceeded before all things to create the elves, so that there might exist reasonable beings to gaze out from their clefts and bur-rows in wonder and reverence at His marvels within the earth. Furthermore, it is known that at a later time this little race un-dertook to exalt itself and to assume dominion over the earth. Wherefore God then created the dragons in order to drive the elves back into the mountains. But since the dragons themselves took care to settle down in the great caves and fissures and to live there, many of them spitting fire and working havoc in many other ways, the elves thus found themselves so hard-pressed and

afflicted that they no longer knew where to come or go. Therefore they turned in humility and supplication to God, the Lord,
calling out to Him and praying Him to exterminate this un-
clean breed of dragons. Yet, if in His wisdom He might not
decide to destroy His own creatures, still the great plight of the
poor elves so touched His heart that at once He created the giants
who were to fight the dragons and if not to root them out, at
least to reduce their number.

'But scarcely had the giants almost disposed of the dragons
than their pride and presumption mounted, in consequence of
which they too committed many atrocities, especially against
the good little elves. These in their extremity turned again to the
Lord. Then He in the might of His power created the knights
who were to fight the giants and the dragons and live harmoni-
ously with the elves. With this the work of creation was ended
upon earth, and it came to pass thereafter that giants and dragons as well as knights and elves were able to coexist and bear
with one another. From which you may infer, my friend, that
ours is the oldest race in the world – an honour, no doubt, but
one that brings us great disadvantages too.

'For since, as you know, nothing persists forever on this
earth but, on the contrary, that everything which has once been
great must become small and less than it was, so it was in our
case; since the beginning of the world we have continued to
grow smaller and to fall away, and the royal family, because of
the purity of its blood, was first and foremost to be subjected to
this fate. Therefore, many years back, our wise men conceived
of a plan to extricate us from our difficulty: from time to time a
princess of the royal house was to be sent out into the world
to take in marriage some honourable knight so that the race
of pygmies might be rejuvenated and saved from complete de-
cline.'

As my lovely one spoke these words with complete candour, I
looked at her uncertainly, because it seemed to me that she
wished to play a little on my credulity. Concerning her dainty
ancestry I had no further doubt; but it caused me some misgiv-
ings that she had seized on me instead of a knight, for I knew

myself too well to be able to believe that my forebears had been directly created by God.

Concealing my amazement and doubt, I asked her kindly: 'But tell me, my dear child, how do you come to have this tall and imposing form? For I know few women to compare with you in fineness of figure!' 'That you shall learn,' said my beauty. 'From olden times we have been advised through the council of the elf-king to beware of taking this extraordinary step as long as possible, which to me seems natural and right. In all probability there would still have been much reluctance to sending a princess out into the world again, had not my younger brother been born so tiny that the nurses actually let him slip through his swaddling clothes and he was lost, and nobody knows what became of him. In this emergency, hitherto quite unheard of in the annals of the elf-kingdom, our wise men were called together, and to make a long story short, they took a resolution to send me out to look for a husband.'

'A resolution!' I cried. 'That is all well and good. One may decide something for oneself, one may decree something for another, but to give a pygmy the stature of a goddess! How did your wise men accomplish that?'

'It was already provided for by our ancestors,' she said. 'In the royal treasury lay an enormous gold finger-ring. – I speak of it now as it appeared in the past when it was shown me, a child, in its natural surroundings; for it is the very same one that I have here on my finger. – At this point they went to work in the following manner: I was informed of everything that awaited me and was instructed what to do and what not to do.

'A magnificent palace, patterned after my parents' favourite summer residence, was constructed; a main building with side wings and everything one could wish for. It stood at the entrance to a large rocky ravine, adding greatly to its beauty. On the appointed day the court assembled there together with my parents and myself. The army was on parade, and twenty-four priests with no little difficulty bore the wonderful ring upon a precious barrow. It was placed upon the threshold of the building, just inside where one would step over it. Many ceremonies were performed and, after an affectionate leavetaking I set to work. I stepped forward, laid my hand upon the ring, and at once began noticeably to increase in size. In a few moments I had attained my present height, whereupon I put the ring upon my finger. Now, in a trice, windows, doors and gates closed up, the wings at either side drew back into the main building, and near me, instead of a palace, stood a small casket which I at once picked up and took along with me, not without an agreeable sensation in being so large and strong. While yet a pygmy, to be sure, in comparison with trees and mountains, with streams and stretches of land, I was, however, a giant in comparison with grass and herbs, but especially with the ants who, since we pygmies were not always on good terms with them, took frequent occasion to plague us.

'How I fared on my pilgrimage before I met you, of this I might have much to tell. It will suffice to say that I put many to the test, but no one except yourself seemed to me worthy of refreshing and perpetuating the line of the sovereign Eckwald.'

This recital gave some occasion for headshaking, although I forebore to shake mine. I put various questions to which, however, I received no direct answers, but instead I learned to my great distress that after what had happened it was necessary for her to return to her parents. Certainly, she hoped to come back to me, but for the moment it was unavoidable that she present herself; otherwise all would be lost for her as well as for me. Soon the purses would cease paying, and all sorts of other consequences might follow.

Upon hearing that our money might give out, I made no further inquiries as to what else might happen. I shrugged my shoulders and said nothing, as she seemed to understand me.

Together we packed up and seated ourselves in the carriage, and opposite to us was the casket in which I could still not discern anything resembling a palace. And so we went on passing many places. Money for lodging and gratuities was easily and generously paid from the pockets to right and left, till at last we arrived at a mountainous region, where scarcely had we alighted than my lovely one went on ahead and I, at her behest, followed with the casket. She guided me up a rather steep footpath to a narrow strip of meadow through which a clear stream, now leaping, now loitering, wound its way. There she called my attention to a flat elevation, directed me to set down the case, and said: 'Fare you well; you will easily find the way back; think of me, I hope to see you again.'

At this moment it seemed to me impossible to leave her. She was just having one of her good days again, or, if you like, her good hours. To be alone with so lovable a creature on the greensward, amid grass and flowers, hemmed in by rocks, soothed by the sounds of water, what heart could have remained unmoved? I wished to take her hand, to clasp her in my arms, but she pushed me back although most affectionately, threatening me with great peril if I did not leave at once.

'Is there not the remotest chance of my remaining,' I cried, 'of your keeping me with you?' I accompanied these words with such gestures and sounds of lamentation that she seemed touched, and after some reflection admitted that it was not entirely impossible for our union to continue. Who was happier than I? My importunity, which became more and more pressing, obliged her to speak out and tell me that, if I could decide to join her in being as small as I had already seen her, it was still not too late for me to remain with her, and pass over with her into her dwelling, her kingdom and her family. This prospect was not altogether pleasing to me; yet at this moment I could not quite tear myself away from her, and since for a considerable time I had been accustomed to the marvellous, and committed to hasty decisions, I assented, telling her she could do with me what she wished.

Thereupon I had to stretch out the little finger of my right hand; she placed her own against it, and drawing off the gold ring very gently with her left hand let it slip onto my finger. Scarcely had she done so when I felt a sharp pain in the finger; the ring contracted, torturing me horribly. I let out a scream and groped around me involuntarily for my lovely one, but she had vanished. My feelings in the meantime were inexpressible, and nothing more remains to be said than that very soon I found myself in a small, compact body near to my charmer in a forest of grass-blades. The joy of reunion after so short and yet so strange a parting or, if you prefer, a reunion without parting, passes all comprehension. I fell upon her neck, she returned my embraces, and the little couple felt as happy as the big one.

With some discomfort we set out to climb a hill; for the grassy meadow had become for us almost impenetrable forest. But finally we reached a clearing, and how astonished I was to see there a large, symmetrical mass, which I was soon forced to recognize as the casket, in the same condition in which I had set it down.

'Go, my friend, and merely knock on it with the ring,' said my sweetheart. 'You will behold wonders.' I walked up to it, and scarcely had I knocked before I witnessed the greatest marvel. Two side wings jutted out, and at the same time, like a shower of scales and shingles, various portions fell into place, revealing a complete palace, equipped with doors, windows and arcades.

A person who has seen one of Röntgen's ingenious writing-tables, so made that a slight tug brings into play a number of ratchets and springs, whereby desk, writing materials, drawers for letters and money come to view either simultaneously or one right after the other, will be able to picture to himself the unfolding of this palace into which my sweet companion now drew me. In the main hall I at once recognized the hearth which I had formerly glimpsed from above, and the chair on which she had sat. And when I looked overhead I thought I could still detect something of the rift in the dome through which I had looked in. I spare you a description of the rest; it is enough to say that all was spacious, costly and in good taste. Scarcely had I recovered from my amazement when I heard from afar the strains of martial music. My lovely half sprang up for joy and rapturously announced to me the approach of her royal father. We went and stood in the doorway and watched while a brilliant procession filed out of a high, rocky cleft. Soldiers, ser-

vants, household officials, and a shining array of courtiers
followed one behind the other. At last we saw a gleaming gal-
axy and in its midst the king himself. When the whole procession had drawn up before the palace, the king advanced with
his personal retainers. His affectionate daughter ran to meet
him, dragging me along; we threw ourselves at his feet; he
raised me most graciously, and it was only when I came to stand
before him that I noticed that in this miniature world I was the
most imposing in stature. Together we went towards the palace,
where the king in the presence of his whole court, addressed us
in a well-prepared speech; expressing his astonishment at find-
ing us here, he bade us welcome, acknowledged me as his son-
in-law, and set the following day for the marriage rites.

How terribly depressed I felt at the mention of marriage! for
hitherto I had dreaded this almost more than music itself, which
otherwise seemed to me the most hateful thing on earth. 'Those
people who make music,' I was wont to say, 'at least remain
under the illusion of being at one with each other, and of working in unison: for when they have been tuning up long enough,
rending our ears with all manner of discords, they are firm and
fast in the conviction that their difficulties have been solved, and
that one instrument is exactly in tune with the other.' Even the
director shares this happy delusion, and delightedly they start
off, while the rest of us feel our ears buzzing from the constant
din. In the wedded state, on the other hand, even this is not the
case: for although it is only a duet, which would lead one to
assume that two voices, or rather two instruments, are bound to
be brought into some degree of harmony, yet this seldom comes
to pass. For if a man leads off with one tone, his wife at once
takes a higher one; in this way they pass from chamber to choral
pitch, on and on, getting higher and higher, until even the wind
instruments cannot follow. Therefore, since even harmonic music remains so offensive to me, it is still less conceivable that I
should suffer the inharmonic.

Of the many festivities to which the day was given there is
not much of which I would or can speak; for I paid them scant
attention. The sumptuous food, and delicious wines, nothing of

this was to my taste. I speculated and pondered on what I should do. Yet I could think of little. I resolved that when night came I would make short work of getting up and going off to hide somewhere. I succeeded in reaching a crevice in the rock into which I squirmed, concealing myself as well as I was able. My next care was to get the unlucky ring off my finger, in which I was not at all successful. On the contrary, I was made to feel that whenever I thought to take it off the ring became tighter, giving me acute twinges of pain, which subsided as soon as I desisted from my purpose.

I awoke in the early morning – for my little body had slept very well – and was on the point of looking around me a bit further when it seemed as if it had begun to rain. For something like sand or grit fell in large quantities through the grass, leaves and flowers; but how terrified I was when everything about me came alive, and an endless swarm of ants rushed down upon me. No sooner had they become aware of me than they attacked me from all sides, and though I defended myself well and courageously, yet finally they so overwhelmed, pinched and pricked me that I was glad when I heard myself called on to surrender. In truth, I did surrender at once, at which an ant of unusual size approached me with politeness, not to say reverence, and even commended himself to my favour. I found that the ants were allies of my father-in-law, and that he had called upon them for aid in the present crisis, and pledged them to bring me back. Small though I was, I was now in the hands of those still smaller. I had to face the wedding and even to thank God if my father-in-law were not in a rage and my lovely one grieved with me.

Permit me to pass over the ceremonies in silence; it is enough to say that we were married; yet though we were gay and lively as the days passed, there were, despite this, some lonely hours in which, being led to reflection, I encountered something I had never encountered before. What it was and how it came about you shall hear.

Everything around me conformed fully to my present shape and needs; the bottle and glasses were well-proportioned to a small drinker, indeed, much better on the whole than ours. To my small gums the delicate morsels had an unparalleled flavour, a kiss from my wife's dainty mouth was too enchanting for words, and I do not deny that novelty made all these associations highly pleasurable. Withal, I had unhappily not forgotten my previous state of existence. I felt within myself a measure of my former greatness, which made me unhappy and restless. Now, for the first time, I grasped what philosophers mean by their ideals, with which man is said to be so afflicted. I had an ideal of myself, and often in dreams I appeared to myself as a giant. In short, the wife, the ring, the dwarfed figure, and many other bonds made me so thoroughly and completely wretched that I began to give earnest thought to my deliverance.

As I was convinced that the whole magic lay in the ring, I determined to file it off. For this purpose I took several files from the court jeweller. Fortunately, I was left-handed and had never in my life done anything by rights. I held myself resolutely to my task; it was not slight: for the golden circlet, although it appeared so thin, had grown thicker in contracting from its former size. I gave all my leisure hours unobserved to this business, and when the metal was nearly filed through I was clever enough to step outside the door. This was well-advised; for all at once the golden circle sprang forcibly from my finger and my body shot up into the air with such vehemence that I really thought I had struck the sky, and in any case I should have broken through the dome of our summer palace, indeed, should have wrecked the entire pavilion with my brusque helplessness.

There I stood again, certainly much bigger, but also, it seemed to me, far more bewildered and ungainly. When I had recovered from my dizziness, I saw lying near me the casket which felt rather heavy as I lifted it and trudged with it down the foot-path towards the post-tavern, when I immediately called for the horses and started travelling. On the way, I was not long in trying the pockets on either side. In place of the money, which seemed to have given out, I found a small key which fitted the casket, in which I found a fair compensation. As long as this lasted I used the carriage; afterwards I sold it in order to be able to go on by the stage-coach. The casket was the last to be disposed of, for I kept thinking it ought to fill itself once more. And so I came at last, though by a somewhat devious way, back to the hearth and the cook, where first you came to know me.